earth
care
books

Eat Up!

Healthy Food for a Healthy Earth

By Candace Savage
Illustrated by Gary Clement

A FIREFLY BOOK

First published in Canada by Douglas & McIntyre Ltd.

Published in the United States in 1993 by
Firefly Books (U.S.) Inc.
P.O. Box 1338
Ellicott Station
Buffalo, New York 14205

Canadian Cataloguing in Publication Data

Savage, Candace, 1949-
Eat up! healthy food for a healthy earth

(Earthcare books)
Includes index.
ISBN 1-895565-13-8

1. Food - Juvenile literature. 2. Nutrition - Juvenile literature. 3. Food industry and trade - Environmental aspects - Juvenile literature.
I. Clement, Gary. II. Title. III. Series.

TX355.S38 1992 j641.3 C92-093998-8

Special thanks to Denyse LeBlanc, Food Engineer, Agriculture Canada, Moncton, New Brunswick; Renate Oddy, Consumer Education Project, Grant MacEwan Community College, Edmonton, Alberta; Clifford Rouder, Department of Nutrition and Food Management, Syracuse University, Syracuse, New York.

Designed by Michael Solomon
Printed and bound in Hong Kong

Contents

CHAPTER 1

Healthy Food?

There are now about 5,000,000,000 people living on planet Earth. That's five *billion* — so many that it's very hard to think of all of us at once. By the time you are a grown-up, there will be one billion more.

Just try to imagine the mountains of food that five or six billion people eat up. The cereal we go through at breakfast. The apples we need for our lunches. The piles of bread, cheese, hamburgers, carrots, peaches, watermelon, ice cream, cookies and other delicious stuff.

And every single bite of it has come to us from the Earth — from oceans, orchards, gardens and farms all around the world. When a fish is pulled out of the ocean, it brings us the goodness of the salt water and sea air. When an orange is picked from an orange tree, it is packed with goodness from the soil, sun, rain and air. Our bodies take in this goodness and turn it into good health. Food is a gift to us from the Earth and not to be wasted.

The food you eat in just one year probably weighs fifteen to twenty times more than you do!

"My Parents Are Away" Dream Menu

If your parents were out of your hair for a day, what would you choose to eat? Make a list of what you would have for breakfast, lunch and dinner on a perfect day. Do you think this diet would keep you healthy?

Far too many people have forgotten this fact. A lot of the foods in our grocery stores have had their goodness wrecked. Doctors say that some people get heart disease, strokes, cancer, diabetes and other illnesses from eating these damaged foods. When we waste the goodness of our food, we waste the good Earth, too. We also take a chance of wasting our own good health.

Processing Can Be a Blessing!

One reason our food has a hard time keeping us healthy is that much of it may have been "processed" too much before we eat it. It may be cleaned, cored, cut, diced, grated, mixed, peeled, roasted, sifted, sliced, trimmed or whipped. It may have had water taken out of it (frozen concentrated juice) or sugar and water put in (canned fruit). All of these ways of changing food are ways of "processing" it.

Food processing is not always a bad thing. In fact, it can be very important. For example, when milk

comes out of a cow, it contains invisible creatures called germs, or bacteria. If people drink "raw," unprocessed milk, they sometimes become sick because of these bacteria. To keep this from happening, our milk is processed, or pasteurized. This means that it is heated up so that the dangerous bacteria are killed. Because the milk has been processed, we stay healthy.

Or suppose you cooked up a batch of baked beans and left it out on the counter for several days. What would happen? If bacteria from the pot, the air or a stirring spoon got into the crock, the baked beans would go bad. Anyone who ate them could get food poisoning. To keep this from happening, baked beans are often processed, or canned. This means that after they are cooked, they are put into metal cans and sealed up tight to keep bacteria out. Then the cans are heated to kill any bacteria that are already inside. No more bacteria, no more food poisoning!

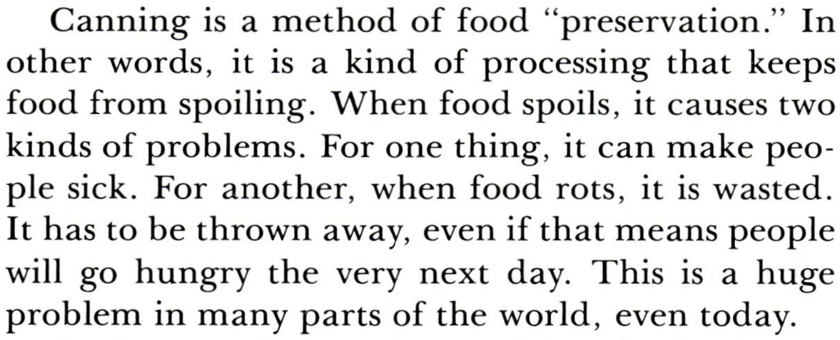

Canning is a method of food "preservation." In other words, it is a kind of processing that keeps food from spoiling. When food spoils, it causes two kinds of problems. For one thing, it can make people sick. For another, when food rots, it is wasted. It has to be thrown away, even if that means people will go hungry the very next day. This is a huge problem in many parts of the world, even today.

Food processing was invented hundreds of years ago because people needed ways to preserve food. Instead of standing by and watching their grapes rot, they learned how to make them into wine or dry them as raisins. They smoked fish (kippered herring) and pickled vegetables (dill pickles). They used salt and spices to preserve meat (beef jerky). If their milk looked as if it might go sour, they quickly made it into yoghurt or cheese.

Processing can also make food more fun to eat. Suppose somebody gave you a sack of wheat — smooth, hard, golden kernels of whole wheat. How would you eat it? You could have it boiled like rice, or boiled like rice, or boiled like rice again. But if the wheat was processed, or ground, into flour, it would suddenly become much more interesting. Now you could mix it up and shape it into long skinny loaves or fat round ones. You could make cakes, bagels, cinnamon buns and dozens of other good things.

Food processing is important. But it's a bit like playing in the sand. To build a sandcastle, you have to "process" the sand (dig it, wet it, pat it, mold it) to get the shape you want. But if you "overprocess" the sand by working on it too long, the towers and turrets of your castle start to crumble.

The same thing happens with food. A certain amount of processing can make food better for us.

Food can be processed by

baking
beating
boiling
brewing
canning
churning
cleaning
coloring
cooking
cooling
creaming
curing
drying
flaking
flavoring
folding
freezing
frying
grating
grinding
heating
icing
kneading
microwaving
pasteurizing
peeling
popping
puffing
refrigerating
rolling
salting
separating
squeezing
sweetening

But if we process it too much, it breaks down and loses its power to keep us healthy.

Processing Can Be Depressing!

Even when food processing is done for a good reason, it always causes some harm. With every change that a food goes through, it loses a little bit of its natural goodness. The more things that have been done to a food before you eat it, the less good it will be able to do for your body.

Think again of that sack of wheat. You could grind the kernels into whole-wheat flour. When grain is processed this way, it loses some of the goodness that was in the kernels. But because the wheat hasn't been changed very much, it is still a powerful food.

But suppose the whole-wheat flour was processed again. Say it was sifted, so that the most nutritious parts of the grain were taken out, and then bleached with chemicals. You would end up with a pile of fine powder, or "white flour." White flour has picked up small amounts of the chemicals, or "additives," that were used to bleach it. At the same time, it has lost much of the goodness that was originally in the kernels of wheat. Flour millers often try to make up for this loss by putting a few vitamins back in and calling the flour "enriched," but that is not the right word for it. The label on white flour should really say "impoverished," because so much of its food value has been stolen away from it.

If this impoverished flour is taken to a bakery, it will be processed again. It may be mixed into a sweet dough, cut into doughnut shapes and fried in a vat of hot fat. When this happens, the wheat is changed so much that it loses most of its food power.

Food can be processed in a

bakery
brewery
butcher shop
candy factory
cannery
cheese factory
dairy
dry-milk plant
egg-grading station
fish plant
flour mill
frozen-food plant
kitchen
pasta shop

and many other places! Is food processed in your community? Could you go for a visit?

I used to think it was
so yummy
To stuff that junk into
my tummy!

In fact, because of the extra sugar and fat that have been added to it, it can actually be bad for your health.

There is no big problem with enjoying a doughnut now and then as a special treat. But there *is* a problem with eating a steady diet of foods — doughnuts, potato chips, white bread, "enriched" macaroni, bacon, sugar-coated cereals, ice cream and soft drinks — that have had too much of their goodness processed out and too much "badness" (salt, sugar, fat or additives) processed in.

When a food has been damaged in this way, we say that it is "overprocessed."

Argh! Additives!

Overprocessed foods often contain small amounts of chemicals called additives. Some additives, known as "preservatives," are put into foods to keep them from going bad. Others are added to products such as mayonnaise and ice cream to make them thicker and creamier. Still others add color and flavor to perk up foods that have been processed so much they have become tasteless. Most of us eat dozens or even hundreds of different additives every week.

Are these chemicals bad for our health? No one can be totally sure. We do know that the additives in our food have been tested. The scientists who have done the tests think that most additives are safe for most people to eat. Even though "sodium carboxymethylcellulose" and "propylene glycol alginate" are probably not on your list of favorite foods, they aren't likely to cause big problems if you eat them.

But there are a few common additives that may be more dangerous. When scientists feed these

chemicals to mice or rats in the laboratory, the animals sometimes get cancer. Chemicals that cause cancer in test animals may also cause cancer in us. So why take the chance? Give your body a break and avoid these additives:

- Some artificial sweeteners, which are used in diet pop and other diet foods. Check the label for the words "acesulfame K" or "saccharin."
- Artificial colorings, which are found in many foods, including some breakfast cereals, candies and soft drinks.
- BHA and BHT, two preservatives that are often added to crackers, cereals, vegetable oils and other products.
- Sodium nitrite, a preservative that is used in bacon, wieners and other processed meats.

Whenever these additives are put into a food, their names must be listed on the package. Why not look into it?

These ADDitives are not a plus In fact, they are a big MINUS.

SHED A TEAR, GOOD READER, FOR POOR SYLVESTER SPUD

This is the tragic true-life story of good Sylvester Spud, who started life as a healthy food and ended his days as junk. Can you see from the pictures how Sylvester's story is also sad for the environment? When we grow good food and then ruin it through over-processing, we use up the goodness of the Earth and get nothing to show for it.

1. Sylvester was grown on a farm and came out of the ground packed with food value. He had a lot to offer. If you had eaten him then and there, he would have helped you grow strong muscles or given you the energy to win a race. His greatest ambition was to put his goodness to work by becoming a baked potato.

2. Sadly, Sylvester's noble dream was not to come true. One day, as he was thinking about whether he'd rather be eaten with chives or without, a truck pulled up to the farm and whisked Sylvester off. The next thing he knew, he had been dumped at the door of a potato-chip factory.

3. Alas, poor Sylvester. First he was peeled, and his peels were thrown away. Much of his goodness was thrown in the garbage.

4. Sylvester was sliced, cooked in fat and coated with salt. The heat destroyed more of the vitamins of which he had once been so proud. Worse yet, the fat and salt that were added to him made him a health hazard. Now when someone ate him, he would put an extra strain on that person's heart.

5. Sylvester's chips were packed in a bag. Chemicals were added to the package to keep the chips from getting stale. Sylvester knew that these additives could be bad for people. Poor unhappy Sylvester. Poor unhappy us!

DELICIOUS DEFINITIONS

Additive: A chemical that is added to food to make it smoother, thicker, tastier or more colorful, or to change it in some other way. Some additives help to keep food from rotting. Many additives are probably safe to eat, but a few of the most common ones may be dangerous.

Bacteria: Tiny creatures, so small they cannot be seen, that sometimes cause diseases and spoil food.

Cancer: A serious illness that may sometimes be caused by chemicals, including a few additives.

Fat: Butter, lard, margarine, vegetable oil and many other foods contain fat. Our bodies need some fat, but too much is bad for our health.

Nutritious: Good for your health.

Pasteurize: To heat milk or honey to kill germs.

Preservation: Processing of food so it will keep longer. Pickling, drying, canning and freezing are all methods of food preservation.

Processing: Changing food in some way to preserve it or to get it ready to eat.

Top This!

Instead of potato chips, try snacking on a baked potato. First, scrub up a spud, prick it with a fork, and pop it in the oven or microwave. When the potato is cooked, cut it in half and top it with sprouts, grated carrots, baked beans, or anything else that tickles your tastebuds. Why are baked potatoes a good choice for you and for the Earth?

You Expect Me To Eat *THAT?!*

If you buy a food that comes in a box, bag, jar or can, you can find out what is in it by reading the list of ingredients on the package. Although the list may look confusing at first, it's actually quite simple. Here's all you need to know to get started.

- Most first, least last. The order in which the ingredients are listed is important. The main ingredient (the one there's most of) comes first; the next-most-important comes second, and so on. For example, if a batch of cookies contains two handfuls of sugar, one handful of flour and a pinch of rolled oats, the ingredients will be listed in that order: sugar, flour, rolled oats.
- Ingredients within ingredients. Sometimes the name of an ingredient is followed by a list of other ingredients in brackets. For example, the list might say, "chocolate (sugar, cocoa butter and lecithin)." This means the food contains chocolate, which in turn is made out of sugar, cocoa butter and lecithin.
- Words with special meanings. On a food package, "flour" usually means enriched white wheat flour. Words like "lard," "coconut oil," "hydrogenated oil," "vegetable oil," "hydrogenated vegetable oil," "palm oil," "palm kernel oil" and "shortening" all refer to kinds of fat. Many different words are also used to describe sugar.
- What language is this? The ingredients with long, strange names toward the end of the list are mostly additives. Some of them are vitamins and minerals, which our bodies can use. Others are of no use to our bodies but have been added to the food to change its color, flavor or texture or to keep it from going bad.

THE SENSIBLE SHOPPER'S FIELD GUIDE TO FOOD

Species name: Overprocessed Food, *Edibilius supraprocessus*
Characteristics: Usually sold in boxes, cans, bottles or boxes. May have a long list of ingredients on the package. Often contains extra sugar, salt and fat. May also contain artificial colors, preservatives and other additives. May be "enriched" because so much of its natural goodness has been taken out.
Habitat: Found in grocery stores, restaurants and kitchens everywhere.
Remarks: A serious pest wherever it occurs. Becoming more common. Consider dangerous!

READING THE FINE PRINT

LUNCH TIME, MUNCH TIME! EAT A WHOLE BUNCH TIME!

Two students have brought their lunches to school. Which of them eats more overprocessed foods? Which lunch would you rather eat?

Which lunch is better for the Earth? If you need a clue, turn to pages 36–37.

BE A SUGAR SLEUTH

Sugar is a source of "empty" calories. In other words, it gives us calories, or energy, but it does not provide any of the other nutrients we need to feel great. Our bodies do not need empty calories; they need whole foods, which give us energy and other goodness at the same time.

Unfortunately, some overprocessed foods, such as jam, icing-filled cookies and ice cream, contain so many "empty" sugar calories that they cannot possibly help us stay healthy. Our foods are often so over-sweetened that sugar comes first or second in the list of ingredients. But even when it isn't first, it sometimes ought to be. This is because different sorts of sugar can be listed under different names, such as "icing sugar," "malt sugar," "maltodextrin," "invert sugar," "sucrose," "corn syrup," "corn syrup solids," "fructose," "fructose-glucose," "polydextrose," "dextrose," "lactose" and others. If all these sweeteners were lumped together as plain sugar instead of being listed one by one, "sugar" would move much higher on the list.

When each kind of sugar is listed separately, we are sometimes tricked into thinking that our food is better for us than it really is. Don't be fooled. Read the fine print. See how many kinds of sugar have been hidden in your food.

Winners and Losers

If overprocessed foods can hurt us, why are there so many of them in our restaurants and grocery stores? Why do stores sell peanut butter that contains sugar and salt when plain ground-up peanuts would be better for our health? Why do we have "drink crystals" made of sugar and additives instead of fruit juice? Why do we hear on TV that eating a big bowl of sugar-frosted rainbow-colored Cruncho Cereal is the only way to get our day off to a decent start?

And why is the problem getting worse? Why, year by year, is more and more of our food being overprocessed?

DELICIOUS DEFINITIONS

Enriched: A food that has had vitamins or minerals added to it. Often the vitamins and minerals that are added as "enrichment" do not make up for the goodness that was lost during processing.

Ingredients: Foods that are mixed together to make other, more complicated foods. A recipe is a list of ingredients.

Nutrient: Something you need to get from your food in order to stay healthy.

Overprocessed: A food that has had too much natural goodness taken out and too much badness (fat, sugar, salt and additives) put in.

Preservative: An additive that helps to keep food from going bad.

Profit: Money that a company earns by selling its products. Companies make the most profit by spending as little as possible to make their products and charging as much as they can when they sell them.

One answer is that the companies that produce overprocessed foods are not in business for the sake of your health. They are in business to make money. The more food they can sell us, the more money they will earn. If the foods they sell us are processed instead of plain, they can charge more for them and make a profit. (A bag of potato chips, for example, costs about twenty times more than the same weight of fresh potatoes.) For the big food companies, selling food is a money game.

To win at the money game, these companies have to sell as much as they possibly can. Each one hopes to take business away from the others by making its own products look extra special. So if one company processes corn to make corn chips, another may try to outdo it by producing corn bugles, rings, curls, puffs, bits and twists. They may add flavors and colors to make their products look more glamorous. Who cares if the food's goodness is wasted in the process? The only real question is, will people buy it?

Unfortunately, the answer to this question is almost always "yes." Some people are willing to purchase even the most worthless food products. Every year, people are buying more foods that are highly processed.

When we choose overprocessed foods, we help the big food companies win at the money game. But by making them into winners, we make losers of ourselves.

A fast-food cheeseburger, with french fries, a shake and apple pie, loads you down with 2 times more calories, 3 times more fat and 4 times more salt than you would get from a healthy meal. People who eat a steady diet of this kind of food are more likely to develop bad hearts and other health problems when they grow up.

A FEW FAST

Fast food isn't necessarily bad food. In fact, pizzas and submarine sandwiches can be fast and nutritious, too. But most foods sold by fast-food restaurants are not very good for you.

A cheeseburger, with fries, apple pie and a shake, sounds like an excellent lunch. After all, you're getting bread, beef, lettuce, tomatoes, cheese, apples, milk and potatoes, which are all good for you. But most fast-food restaurants spoil this goodness by processing the food in an

FACTS FOR FAST-FOOD FANS

unhealthy way. They put in too much sugar, too much fat, too much salt and too many additives. They do not make sure that their meals provide enough vitamins.

Fast food is fun, and everyone wants to eat it now and again. So here's how to choose a healthy meal on your next fast-food break.

- Buy pizza or sandwiches instead of burgers or chicken. Choose vegetable toppings such as tomatoes, mushrooms and green peppers instead of pepperoni, bacon or sliced meat. Ask to have your sandwich made on whole-grain bread.
- Choose barbecued chicken instead of fried chicken, fingers or nuggets.
- Have a baked potato instead of fries.
- Order a salad with your meal.
- Choose milk or juice instead of a shake or soft drink.

CHAPTER 2

Healthy Earth?

Read this chapter to learn about problems in our food system. Then turn to Chapter 3 for some answers!

Whenever you put something into your mouth, you are taking it on the last small step of a long complicated journey that may have begun months before and covered half the Earth. The journey began when the food was grown — in a lake, or on a ranch or farm. From there the food traveled to a factory where it was processed and put into packages. After that, it traveled some more, to your grocery store, to your kitchen and, finally, to your fork.

This process, which brings food to your plate, is called the "food system."

Our food system is a success in many important ways. For example, it keeps our grocery stores filled to the brim day after day. But the modern food system has its weaknesses, too. For one thing, it produces too many overprocessed foods. At the same time, our food system also "overprocesses" the Earth by using up too much of its natural goodness, or resources.

Did you know that

- every year, we lose a little bit more good topsoil that we need for growing food;
- we are using up fuels such as gasoline that we need to run tractors, trucks and food-processing plants;
- pollution from our vehicles and machines is causing the planet to get hotter, because of the Greenhouse Effect. Will our crops still be able to grow if the climate of the Earth is badly damaged?

Do You Eat Gas for Lunch?

Of course you don't eat gasoline, not really. But without knowing it, you rely on gasoline and other sources of energy to provide your food. In a way, there's a bit of gasoline in everything you eat.

Think of a glass of orange juice. Once upon a time, that sweet delicious liquid was inside an orange, hanging on an orange tree in an orange grove. To make juice for you, somebody had to plant the tree and care for it, wait for the oranges to ripen, pick them at just the right time and drive them to an orange-juice factory. There, other people used machines to squeeze the juice out and get it ready for canning or freezing. Then still more people packed the juice into cartons and shipped it to warehouses in your town or city. Then another crew of people loaded it up and trucked it from the warehouse to your neighborhood store so it would be there when you went to shop.

Every time anything was done to the orange, whether it was being grown, squeezed, canned, frozen or trucked, energy was used. Most of the energy to do this work came from gasoline. Gasoline is a fossil fuel, which means it was formed from the

With the amount of fuel that we use to produce one loaf of bread (to grow the wheat, grind the flour, bake the bread and transport it), people in some other countries could produce fifty loaves. The difference is that we use fuel to run machines and transport our bread over long distances. They use more muscle-power and eat bread that was produced locally.

bodies of creatures that died long ago and were buried inside the Earth. After thousands of years, these bodies turned into a black tarry goo that we call "crude oil." We pump the crude oil out of the ground and refine it to make plastics, medicines, heating oil, diesel fuel and gasoline.

There are two big problems with burning up so much fuel to run our food system. One is that fossil fuels are "nonrenewable." This means that the faster we use them up, the sooner they'll be gone. The other problem is that burning fossil fuels causes pollution. When we burn gasoline, we send exhaust into the air, where it causes smog and adds to "global warming." The more energy we use, the worse these problems will get.

If everybody in the world used as much energy as we do to produce food, all the crude oil would be gone in about thirteen years.

It takes the energy of 10 tanks of gasoline to feed you for one year. That's about 500 liters or 130 U.S. gallons. How much energy would our food system use to feed all 5,000,000,000 people on Earth?

FILL 'ER UP!

Our food system uses the energy of about half a tank of gasoline to grow, process, package and transport one grocery cart of food. (Some of this energy is used in the form of electricity, but to keep things simple we'll talk about it as if it all came from gasoline.) You probably eat about twenty carts of food each year. How much energy have you "eaten up" in your lifetime?

If you're not in the mood for figuring, you can look up the answer on this chart. How much energy will it take to feed you until you are grown-up? Until you're a grandparent?

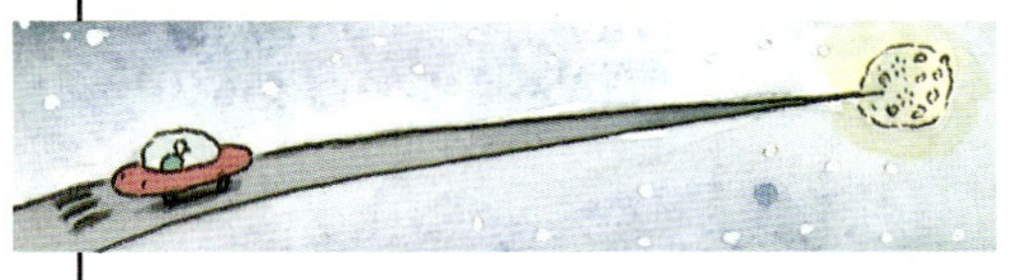

Age	Carts of Food	Tanks of Gas
5	100	50
6	120	60
7	140	70
8	160	80
9	180	90
10	200	100
11	220	110
12	240	120
20	400	200
30	600	300
40	800	400
80	1,600	800

- Placed end to end, 1,600 grocery carts would form a line twelve blocks long.
- If you could drive to the moon, 800 tanks of gas would take you all the way there.

Down on the Farm

When your grandmother and grandfather were children, there wasn't a complicated food system. There was just food. Most people lived on farms and grew what they needed themselves. If your grandfather wanted an omelet for breakfast, he didn't go to the superstore. He went to the chicken coop and pulled an egg out from under a hen. For milk, your grandmother went to the cow barn, sidled up beside old Bossy and squeezed on her udder until the milk streamed out. To get flour, your great-grandfather hitched up his work horses and planted corn or wheat, which he later took to a flour mill to be ground. Apples came from the tree behind the house and, if you wanted a snack, you walked over and pulled one down.

No packaging. No processing. No transportation. Very little fuel was used to grow and handle food. People had always lived like this, for hundreds and thousands of years.

Then, about the time your mom and dad were kids — just an eye blink ago in the history of the Earth — things started to change. People began moving off the farms and into the cities and towns. They took jobs in offices and factories. They no longer had enough land or time to grow food for themselves.

Out in the country, things were changing, too. The people who were left on the farms got rid of their horses and bought tractors, which had just been invented. With the help of these machines, fewer people could grow more food than ever before. Soon the farmers were buying bigger tractors and bigger trucks and bigger harvesters. They bought farm chemicals such as fertilizers, insect poisons and weed-killers, which helped them to grow even more. Before long, a few farmers were producing enough for themselves and all the people in the cities, too.

Of the ten tanks of gas that it takes to feed you for one year, four tanks are used on the farms where your food is grown.

Grow more food! Plow up more meadows. Cut down more trees. Drain more marshes and ponds. Plant more land to crops. Burn up more gasoline. Use up more fuel to make farm chemicals.

Soon people were up to their ears in good things to eat. But in the rush to grow more food, they sometimes forgot to care for the soil, which was gradually losing its natural goodness. They were destroying marshes and forests where animals raised their young and birds made their nests. They were poisoning the Earth with farm chemicals and polluting the air with exhaust from tractors and farm machines. They were using up huge quantities of

WHAT'S THE BEEF WITH MEAT?

One reason our diet is hard on the Earth is that we eat more meat than our great-grandparents did. To produce meat, we first grow grain and hay to feed to meat-producing animals such as cows, pigs, sheep and chickens. Planting and harvesting this animal food uses up energy and other resources.

When the animals eat the food, they turn it into beef, pork, mutton and chicken drumsticks. But, unfortunately, they have to eat a lot of food to produce a little meat. A chicken, for example, has to eat about twice its weight in grain. A pig eats four times its weight in grain. A beef cow eats eight times its weight in grain. This means that when you have a small piece of fried chicken, you are "eating up" all the energy that went into growing a big pile of chicken feed. When you have roast beef, you are eating up the energy that went into growing an even larger pile of cow feed.

Our meaty diet puts an extra strain on the Earth. But does this mean that we should all stop eating meat and become vegetarians? For most people, the answer is "probably not." Meat is a valuable food; it gives us vitamins, minerals and protein that we need for good health. It takes careful thought and study to stay healthy without it.

But most of us eat more meat than we need. So when you have dinner, take a smallish pork chop instead of a huge one. When you make your lunch, put peanut butter in your sandwiches instead of bologna. Make spaghetti sauce without meat and serve it with whole-wheat noodles and cheese. Celebrate Meat-free Mondays. Eat more fish, chicken and turkey, and less pork and beef. Eat more corn, wheat, rice, beans, eggs, cheese and other "meat substitutes."

Doctors say that our meat-hungry habits are hurting our health, so by cutting back on the amount we eat, we are helping the Earth and ourselves.

nonrenewable fuels, which would never be there for people to use again.

This is still the way most of our food is grown. Whether you bite into a hotdog or a cookie or a peanut-butter sandwich, you are biting into some of these farm problems — sick soil, polluted water and wasted energy. That's pretty hard to swallow, isn't it?

OUR FOOD SYSTEM IS GREEDY FOR ENERGY BECAUSE

- we use big farm machines and large amounts of fertilizer to grow food (making fertilizer uses up a lot of fossil fuels);

- we eat too much meat;

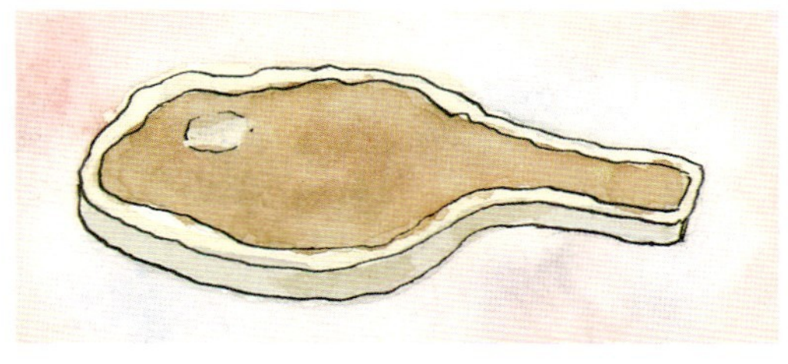

- we transport our food over long distances;

- we use energy to make unnecessary packaging.

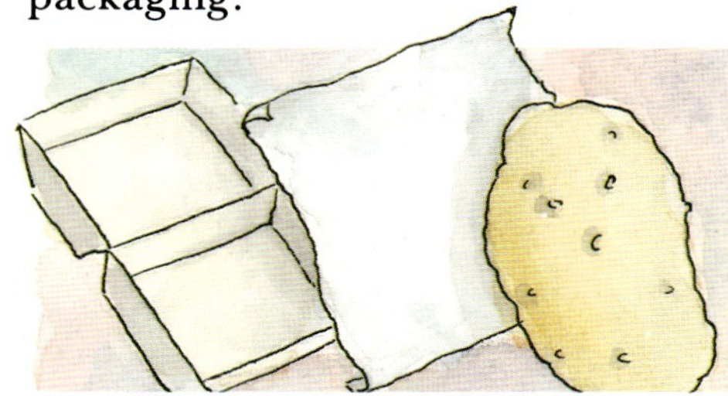

Go Shopping and See the World

Our food system uses almost as much energy to store and move our food around after it is grown as it does to grow the food in the first place. Some of this energy-cost is necessary — we have to get our food from where it is produced to where we live. Unless you want to spend your entire life sitting beside a cow, for example, somebody has to burn a little gas to bring milk to you. But it makes sense to keep the distances as short as possible. The less our food travels, the less fuel we have to burn and the less pollution we create.

Of the ten tanks of gas that it takes to feed you for one year, three tanks are used to transport your food from the farm to the processing plants and on to the grocery store.

Unfortunately, this sensible rule is often broken. Many foods in our grocery stores have traveled for hours or even days to get to us. For example, the potatoes in your order of french fries may have been grown on the other side of the continent, when they literally could have come from your own backyard. Or the apple in your lunchbox may have been shipped all the way across the ocean, even though apples can be grown much closer to your home.

The journeys taken by our food are getting longer every year. In a way, this is great. It's fun to walk into the grocery store and see bananas from the tropics, oranges from the sunny south, kiwi fruit from New Zealand, chocolate from Africa and bottled water from France. It's fun, but it's terribly extravagant. Do we have the right to hurt the Earth just to give our tastebuds a thrill?

PUT YOUR BREAKFAST ON THE MAP

When you stagger out for breakfast, still not quite awake, foods from half-way around the world may be waiting on your plate. Do you ever eat any of the foods in this breakfast? Where do you suppose they were grown? The answers may surprise you!

To find out where your breakfast comes from, look for signs on the bins and boxes of fruits and vegetables at the grocery store. Check for addresses on packages that other foods come in. If that doesn't help, look in the encyclopedia.

When you've learned as much as you can about your favorite foods, get a map of the world or make a quick tracing from an atlas. Draw little pictures on the map to show where each of the foods comes from.

Preserve Us From Too Much Preserving!

Preserving food takes energy. When foods are canned, for example, they must be heated to a high temperature and kept steaming hot for half an hour, an hour, or even longer. When vegetables are frozen, they are first heated in boiling water or steam, then quick-chilled and put through a freezer tunnel. In both cases, heating and cooling the foods uses up large amounts of energy. Keeping foods frozen after they have been processed also burns up energy.

In fact, every kind of food processing takes some energy. The more steps a food goes through, the more energy is consumed. For example, a certain amount of energy is needed to turn milk into Cheddar cheese. If the Cheddar cheese is then made into processed cheese, more energy is used. If the processed cheese is made into cheese spread, even more is consumed. And as we use more energy, we leave less goodness in the food.

FUEL IN, FOOD OUT

Different methods of preserving foods use up different amounts of energy. Which method of preservation takes the least energy? Which requires the most? If the arrow points to F (Full), that means very little energy was used. If it points to E (Empty), more energy was used to preserve the food.

Throwaways Should Go Away!

Huge amounts of energy and other resources are also used to make packaging. Paper packages, such as boxes and bags, are made from trees that have been chopped out of the forests. Plastic packages, such as bottles, tubs and foam trays, are made from crude oil that has been pumped out of the ground. "Tin" cans are made from iron that has been mined from the Earth and refined into steel. Glass jars are made out of sand that has been melted at high temperatures. All these processes pollute the soil, water and air and, in other ways, spoil the beauty of our home planet.

The Earth pays a big price to provide us with packages. Yet, all too often, once they are made, we treat them as if they were trash. Most food packages are made to be used once and then chucked. In just one year, an average person throws away about eighty cans of garbage. About one-third of

Of the ten tanks of gas that it takes to feed you for a year, three tanks are used to process your food and put it in packages.

them — more than twenty-five garbage cans — are crammed with food packages.

Most people understand that we have to stop wasting so much. But some of our food companies are making it hard for us. Instead of using less packaging, they are giving us even more. Cheese slices with throwaway wrappers. Pudding in throwaway cups. Microwave dinners on throwaway dishes. Juice in throwaway boxes, with their own throwaway straws.

The companies that package our food this way say that they are giving us what we want. They say that we want throwaway packages because they are more "convenient." But how convenient will it be to live on the Earth if everything has been spoiled? Our throwaway habits are throwing away the future!

DELICIOUS DEFINITIONS

Calorie: A little bit of energy. Just as centimeters and inches are used to measure length, calories are used to measure energy.

Energy: Get-up-and-go. Gasoline and electricity provide energy for our machines. Food provides energy for our bodies.

Fertilizer: Chemicals that are put on soil to help plants grow.

Food system: The journey that food takes from where it is grown to where it is processed, where it is sold and, finally, where it is eaten.

Fossil fuel: Gasoline, diesel fuel, heating oil, propane, coal and natural gas.

Greenhouse Effect: A warming-up of the climate of the Earth, caused partly by burning gasoline and other fossil fuels.

Nonrenewable resource: Something that cannot grow back or be replaced after we have used it.

Resources: Things we use to make life better for ourselves. Soil, plants, wind, rain, gasoline, iron and trees are all examples of resources.

Vegetarian: A person who eats grains, beans, nuts, seeds, cheese and other foods, instead of eating meat.

CHAPTER 3

Good for Us!

There are five simple words that can help us choose foods that are good for our health and good for the Earth. They are the "5 N's": Need, Natural, Now, Near and Naked.

Shopping List
Whenever you can, choose foods that
✓ you NEED to be healthy
✓ are NATURAL, or lightly processed
✓ are fresh, or NOW in season
✓ come from NEAR your home
✓ are NAKED, or have little packaging

The First "N": Heed What You Need

"Need" means choosing the foods that help you to grow and stay healthy. To do this, you have to know a little bit about nutrition, the science that tells us what we need to eat. Books about nutrition often seem very complex, full of words like "linoleic acid" and "polysaccharides." But you don't have to master all these details to know what to choose. In fact, you probably already have a pretty clear idea about what is, and is not, good for you.

Nutritionists say that we should follow two easy rules. First, we should go for natural foods — ones that have come through the food system without being greatly changed. Because they have not been overprocessed, these foods have kept most of their power to build good health. They have not been loaded down with extra salt, sugar, fat and additives that can cause problems.

Second, we should treat ourselves to a lot of variety. It is important to eat many different natural foods, as well as different types of them. We need a good balance of fruits, vegetables, nuts, whole grains, milk products and meat. A good diet is not just "meat and potatoes." It is meat, potatoes, cabbage, broccoli, alfalfa sprouts, lettuce, tomatoes, cherries, cantaloupe, apples, yoghurt, eggs, cheese, peanuts, sunflower seeds, vegetable oil, brown rice, whole oats, whole wheat and other natural foods.

To learn more about choosing "natural" foods, just turn the page.

DEAR DIET DIARY . . .

Some morning soon, start the day with a piece of paper and a pencil in your pocket. Every time you eat something, make a note of it. Do this all day long, from breakfast to bedtime. When you have finished, take a good look at what is on your list. Did you eat a variety of natural foods, such as fresh fruits, vegetables, whole grains, nuts, seeds, milk, cheese and meat? Did you eat a lot of foods that contain extra sugar, fat or salt (ice cream, cookies, salted popcorn)? Do many of the foods on your list contain additives, such as food coloring? Is your diet practically perfect, or are there some things you'd like to change?

Nutritionists say that most of us could improve our diets. They say we need to eat

- more fruits and vegetables;
- more whole grains, such as whole-grain bread, whole-grain spaghetti and brown rice;
- more lean meats, such as chicken and fish (and less fatty meat, such as beef and pork);
- fewer foods that contain extra salt, sugar, fat and additives, such as junky snacks and other over-processed products.

If you follow this simple advice, you will be well on your way to good health. And just by doing what's best for you, you are also respecting the Earth. You are making sure that the resources that went into producing your food are put to good use.

The Second "N": Going Natural

"Natural" means choosing foods that look the same (or almost the same) when you eat them as they did when they were grown. These foods may have been cleaned, sorted and packaged, but they have not been changed very much by the food system. When you see them in the grocery store, it is easy to imagine how they looked when they were swimming in the ocean or growing on the farm. Fresh strawberries, watermelon, peaches, pears, celery, corn on the cob, beans, sesame seeds, turkey and shrimp are all examples of whole, natural foods.

The natural-food category also includes foods that have been changed just a little bit by the food system. For example, pasteurized milk is a natural food, because it has gone through only a few steps. It is better than chocolate milk, which has been processed more. Chocolate milk, in turn, is better than a chocolate "shake," which has gone through many more changes. Fresh oranges are better than frozen orange juice concentrate, which is better than frozen juice with sugar added to it.

Going "natural" means choosing plain potatoes instead of frozen french fries. Plain plums instead of plum jam. Plain cheese instead of squeeze-from-the-package cheese spread. Some people think that it means being bored to death, but eating natural foods is not boring at all. Just because you buy your food plain, you don't have to eat it that way. A "plain" old potato can be mashed, scalloped or home-fried. It can be dressed up with pizza spices, shaped into potato cakes or patted into shepherd's pie.

When you buy processed food, it has already been mixed, shaped, colored, flavored and given a name. Somebody else has decided how the food should look, taste, feel and smell. But when you eat natural foods, these choices are left up to you. You're the one who has all the fun of playing around with your food.

Natural foods often have another advantage, too. They are more varied and interesting than processed products. One jar of processed plum jam is pretty much like all the rest. But the fresh natural plums in the produce store come in all sizes and shapes. Some are purple with pointy ends and dry, firm flesh. Others are yellow or green or pink and feel soft when you bite into them. Each kind has its own distinct smell, texture and taste.

The companies that make processed foods spend billions of dollars each year on advertising. Each company wants us to believe that its brand of breakfast cereal, potato chips or cola is very different from the brand made by some other company. In

Please Play with Your Food

Could you drink a strawberry? Put a funny face on a pear? Make a necklace — and eat it?

Could you bake a loaf of whole-wheat bread or create a natural and nutritious pizza?

Eating natural foods can be a lot of fun. All it takes is a little imagination. Why not have a contest at your home or school? See who can make the most interesting or delicious snack using all-natural foods.

fact, different brands are often almost exactly alike. But natural foods give us real variety, the spice of life!

Four good things happen when you choose natural, unprocessed foods. The first is that you have more interesting textures and tastes in your diet. Second, you get all the goodness and good health that your food can give you. Third, your body doesn't have to deal with the extra sugar, fat, salt and additives that are added to processed products. And finally, by eating natural foods, you are being kind to the Earth. It uses less energy and causes less harm to nourish you with healthy food than it would to fill you up with junk.

Farming Nature's Way

Buying natural food can also mean shopping for "organic" fruits and vegetables. Organic farming is a way of growing food without farm chemicals such as fertilizers, weed-killers and insect poisons. These chemicals, which are used every day to grow the food we eat, often make life difficult for wild plants, insects, birds and animals. Some of these chemicals also get into the water and air, where they can hurt all of Earth's creatures, including us. Organic farming prevents these problems by using safer, more

natural ways to care for the soil and control weeds and insects. The methods used by organic farmers are also good for the soil.

Food that was grown on organic farms is usually labeled "organic" or "certified organic." Look for it when you go shopping. It may cost a little more than chemically grown food, but it's worth more, too. (As more people buy organic foods, the price will likely come down.) If you can't find many organic products at your grocery store, speak to the manager or write a letter. Better yet, tell other people — your sisters, brothers, friends, parents, aunts, uncles, teachers — about the problem. One person can't change things alone, but many people can!

SUPER NATURAL NOTIONS

Here are several simple ways to enjoy more natural foods in your diet:

- Catch That Crunch. Have fun with fresh fruits and vegetables. Listen to the crisp snap of your carrot. Stretch the springy strings in your celery. Coddle the cuddly cheek of a peach. SPPPit out watermelon seeds. Are overprocessed foods really more interesting than natural ones, or have we been brainwashed by the ads on TV?

- Make Your Own Munchies. Create a snack mix out of sunflower seeds, peanuts, coconut and raisins. (It's okay to slip in a few chocolate chips.) Eat it instead of candy or chips. Or try whole-grain crackers with peanut butter or cut-your-own cheese. Pop up a pot full of popcorn and flavor it with pizza seasonings or other herbs instead of butter and salt.
- Do Yourself a Flavor Favor. Be willing to try new foods. When you go shopping, look for new varieties of fruits and vegetables. How many of these kinds of apples have you tasted: Red Delicious, Golden Delicious, Newton, McIntosh, Red Rome, Empire, Granny Smith? How many others can you find in the grocery store?
- Stay on the Outside Track. Do most of your shopping along the outside walls of the grocery store, where basic foods such as fresh fruits and vegetables, bread, meat, milk, cheese and eggs are sold. Spend less time on the inner aisles of shelves, which are usually filled with processed and overprocessed foods.
- What's Cooking? Learn to cook. If you don't know a "tsp" from a "tbsp" or a "mL" from an "L," ask one of your parents to teach you the basics. Then check the library for interesting natural-food cookbooks like *The More With Less Cookbook* by Doris Janzen Longacre, *Extending the Table: A World Community Cookbook* by Joetta Handrich Schlabach, *Diet for a Small Planet* by Frances Moore Lappe or *The Enchanted Broccoli Forest* by Mollie Katzen.

CONGRATULATIONS! YOU'VE CHOSEN THE . . .

Here's how to run your own natural-foods taste test.

- Buy two different varieties or pears, such as Anjou and Bartlett. One pear of each kind will be plenty. (If you cannot get pears, use two different kinds of apples, oranges, plums, grapes or tomatoes.)
- Cut one of the pears into bite-sized pieces and put it on a plate. Write the name of the pear (Anjou or Bartlett) on a piece of paper. Set the paper upside down beside the plate so that no one will be able to read it until you show it to them.
- Prepare the other pear, with its name, in exactly the same way.
- Now you are ready to run your test. Ask each person to eat a piece of each pear. As the tester eats each one, ask him or her to describe how it smells, feels and tastes. Are the two kinds of pear very different from one another? Which one does the person like best?

When the person has finished, turn over the pieces of paper, so the tester can learn the name of his or her favorite.

The Third "N": Get Fresh Now

"Now" means eating foods that are fresh or "in season." It means, as much as possible, avoiding foods that have been preserved. We need to do this because the common methods of preserving food use up so much energy. It costs the Earth less to feed us if we choose fresh foods instead of ones that have been canned or frozen. Fresh foods are also better for our health.

Sometimes the "now" rule is easy to follow. For example, it's easy to stop buying frozen or canned carrots because we can always buy fresh ones. But

sometimes the choices are more difficult. Some fresh foods, such as cherries, don't keep very well. We can buy them fresh for a few weeks each year, at cherry-picking time. After that, we can only buy them frozen or in cans. Should we eat these preserved cherries, or should we let them pass?

The "now" rule says we should eat cherries mostly when they are fresh. The rest of the year, we should eat more of the fruits that keep well, such as apples and pears. This means that many of us will have fewer choices in the winter, when fewer foods are fresh. But we will have more variety as we move from winter to spring, spring to summer, summer to fall.

Every season has its own natural taste treats. Fall is special because there are pumpkins. December brings us turkeys and cranberries. Spring has fresh leafy lettuce, little green onions and tangy radishes. Summer offers us peaches, raspberries and fresh corn. If we eat more of our food when it's fresh, we can eat our way through the year and taste each season at its best. At the same time, we will use less energy and be gentler to the Earth.

Does this mean you should never eat food that's been frozen or canned? No, it does not. The sky isn't going to fall if you make a pie out of canned pumpkin in March or enjoy a bowl of frozen strawberries in January. Besides, in the winter time, you may need to eat preserved foods to have a varied, healthy diet. You don't have to be perfect; just do the best you can. If your diet is *mostly* fresh, that's excellent.

The Fourth ''N'': Near and Dear to You

"Near" means choosing more foods that were grown and processed close to where you live. It means thinking twice before choosing foods that have traveled long distances.

Some people are convinced that their bodies need foods that come from faraway places. For example, people who live in cold countries (where oranges cannot grow) often believe they must have oranges or orange juice to give them vitamin C. But this isn't so. They can get all the vitamin C they need from a serving of local cabbage! People in warm countries (where wheat doesn't do well) sometimes believe they must eat bread made of wheat. But this isn't true, either. They can stay just as healthy by eating rice, millet, sorghum or some other grain that grows locally.

Most parts of the world grow an amazing variety of food. Just think of what comes from the gardens and farms close to you. Does fruit grow in your region? (What about berries?) Are there fish in your

lakes? Imagine all those different foods crowded on your plate.

Now change the scene to winter. What grows around you then? In snowy parts of the world, winter foods can be limited. But even in the cold months, we can often get local eggs, milk, cheese, meat or grains. We can even get fresh fruits and vegetables, such as carrots, parsnips, turnips, potatoes, squash, pears and apples. When these crops are harvested in the fall, they are put in special refrigerated buildings where they stay fresh for many months. These storage vegetables and fruits should be the first choice for your winter diet.

If you want more variety — a plate of broccoli or green beans — then you have two good options. One is to eat locally grown food that has been canned or frozen. For example, you might have canned beans or frozen broccoli that grew in your own garden. The other possibility is to buy fresh foods that have been brought in from a not-too-distant place. (If you have a choice, pick the foods that have traveled the shortest distance.) These choices aren't 100 percent perfect, but they still get high marks.

HAVE A LOCAL LUNCH

What kinds of food are produced in or near your community? To find out, ask your parents or friends. Look in a vegetable garden. Shop at the farmers' market. Is there a food co-op nearby that stocks local foods? See if you can make a list of fifty foods that grow in your part of the world.

Sometimes you can buy local foods at the supermarket. If you can't find what you want, ask the manager for help. Tell him or her why you want to eat more local foods. Ask why there are not more of them in your grocery store. Do the manager's explanations make sense to you, or not? If there are real problems, how can they be solved?

Why not have a special meal that features foods that were grown or processed in your community or region? You could do this with your family at home or with your friends at school.

The Fifth ''N'': N-n-n-naked!

"Naked" means choosing foods that come with the least possible amount of packaging. It means avoiding foods that are too dressed up, like the cookies that are sold on plastic trays, inside foil bags, inside cardboard boxes, inside plastic wraps. Some packaging is important, but we clearly don't need all that!

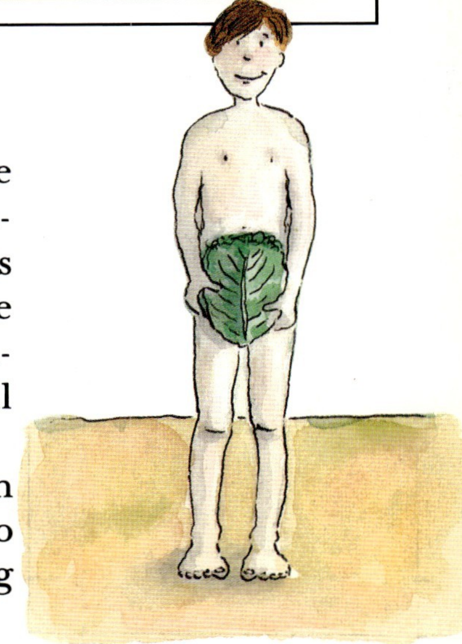

There are three important ways to cut down on packaging. The simplest and best method is to choose foods that are sold with little or no packaging on them. This is called "reducing." The second-best way is to choose packages that can be taken back to the store and filled up again. This is called "reusing." The third-best way is to choose packages that can be collected and made into new products. This is called "recycling."

Here are some easy ways to waste less packaging.

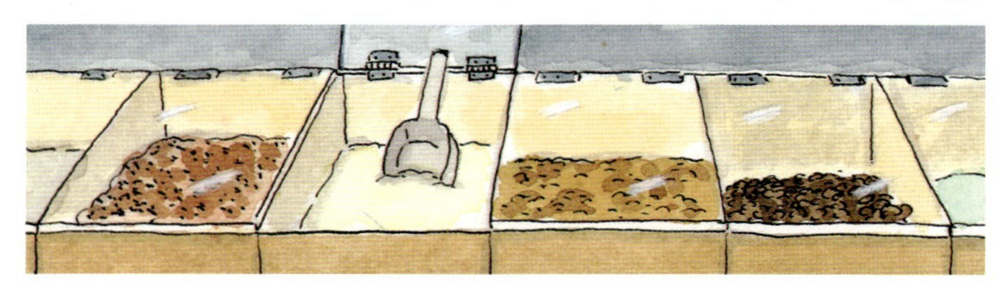

- Bulk is best. Many foods, such as dried peas, beans, nuts, flour, cookies, bagels and buns, can be bought in bulk. Buy them! (Be sure to use the tongs or scoops that are provided, so the food will stay clean.)

Buy fruits and vegetables (tomatoes, mushrooms, green beans) that are free of packaging, rather than those that come in boxes or on trays. Ask the meat department to wrap your meat without cardboard or foam-plastic trays.

- Think big. Buy food in large packages (but not so large the food will spoil before it can be eaten). Do not buy small one-serving packages. It takes more resources to make twenty one-serving packages than to make one large package that holds twenty servings.

• Bring them back. Rinse out your plastic vegetable bags, take them back to the store and use them again. Reuse plastic shopping bags, too, or find ones made of cloth that will serve for years. Try to buy juice, peanut butter, milk and other foods in refillable containers. Take them back to the store for a refill.

If you cannot get food in refillable containers at your supermarket, check out the health food store or food co-op.

• Going around in circles. Choose food in containers that can be recycled. First, find out what materials are recycled in your community. Paper bags? Cardboard boxes? "Tin" cans? Aluminum pop cans? Plastic pop bottles? Plastic tubs? Milk cartons? Where do your recycled materials go, and what is made from them? Are any of them made into new food containers?

When cardboard boxes, glass bottles and plastic tubs are recycled, they are usually not made into food containers. Instead they are made into other products, such as newsprint (paper), pavement (glass) or plastic lumber (plastic). But "tin" cans, aluminum cans and some plastic pop bottles can be recycled and made into new "tin" cans, aluminum cans and pop bottles. The new containers are exactly the same as the old ones. This is called "closed-loop recycling," and it is the best kind.

Eating for the Earth

The "5 N's" — Need, Natural, Now, Near and Naked — are small, simple words, but they call for big changes in the way we choose our food.

You may find that some of the changes are easy to make right now. For example, you may be happy to choose juice in a recyclable can instead of a throwaway box. Or to buy fresh carrots instead of frozen ones. Or to eat pears that grew in your own region instead of mangoes that were shipped in from another country.

But there may be other changes that don't come as readily. Maybe you hate the thought of giving up canned ravioli, or you secretly wish you could eat ice cream with chocolate sauce for breakfast. Or

CHECK OUT THIS CHECKOUT

Here are two shoppers. Which one has chosen more healthy foods? Which one has made choices that are better for the planet? See if you can find at least ten differences, then turn to page 55 for the answers.

perhaps you still find yourself at the junk-food rack as soon as you get your allowance.

Don't give up on yourself if you sometimes make a "wrong" choice. For one thing, there's absolutely nothing wrong with having a treat sometimes. For another, you can't expect the way you eat to change overnight. After all, you have spent your whole life

DELICIOUS DEFINITIONS

Nutrition: The science that studies what we should eat to be in good health. A person who studies nutrition is a nutritionist.

Organic: A kind of farming that avoids using chemicals such as fertilizers, weed-killers and insect poisons. These chemicals can be dangerous to wild plants, insects, birds, animals and people.

Recycling: Collecting used materials and reprocessing them to make new products. When the new product (a new aluminum can) is exactly the same as the old one (a used aluminum can), the process is called "closed-loop recycling."

Reducing: Buying less and throwing away less.

Reusing: Using things over and over again until they are worn out. When we take pop bottles back to the store so they can be filled again, we are reusing them.

getting used to certain foods. As you learn to follow the "5 N's," a world of wonderful new tastes will gradually open to you.

The new world that you enter will be filled with your own good health. It will be filled with hope for the billions of people who live on this planet.

ANSWERS TO "CHECK OUT THIS CHECKOUT"

The shopper on the left has followed the "5 N's" by choosing • reusable shopping bags instead of throwaway ones; • peanut butter in a large refillable tub instead of a smaller throwaway container; • whole-grain pasta in bulk instead of enriched pasta in a can; • whole-grain bread instead of white bread; • fresh cherries in season instead of frozen ones; • hard cheese instead of wrapped processed slices; • fish instead of beef steaks; • local fruits (apples and pears) instead of tropical ones (bananas and pineapples); • healthy snacks (raisins and nuts) instead of cheesies and chips; • orange juice instead of grape drink.

Index